The Story of

The
Sea
Glass

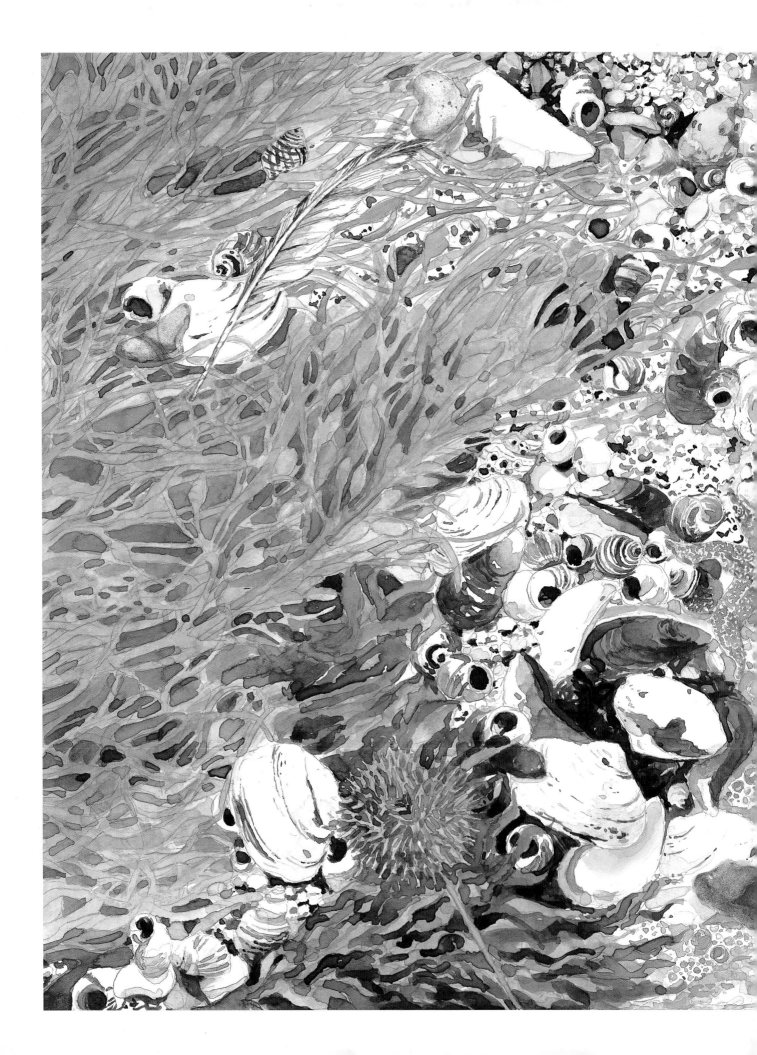

The Story of
The
Sea
Glass

by
Anne Wescott Dodd
illustrated by Mary Beth Owens

"Nana! Nana! I found a shell!" Nicole shouted.

Nana smiled as she watched her granddaughter skip-dance her way back through the sun seekers on the crowded city beach.

Nicole handed a black and somewhat slimy shell to her grandmother. "It's small and a little bit broken."

"But it is a shell," Nana said. "And shells here are very hard to find. Oh, Nicole, how you would love the sea I knew when I was a child!"

"Tell me! Tell me about your island." Nicole loved hearing about long ago and far away—even when her grandmother told the same stories again and again.

Nana leaned back on the beach towel and closed her eyes. "On my island, blue skies seemed to hug the sea. The air was scented with salt and rose. And the raspberries that grew in the thicket beside my house were the sweetest I ever tasted."

"What about the beach, Nana? Tell me about your beach."

"Well, it wasn't a big sandy beach like this. There were only small patches of sand squeezed in among many rocks. But under their seaweed cover, sometimes I found tiny starfish hiding. And when I climbed the rocks or walked at the water's edge, I could be alone with wind and waves and seabirds soaring overhead. The island was such a special place. So many years ago . . . It would be wonderful to see my home again "

"Couldn't we go there?" Nicole asked. "Can we take a trip together when school is out?"

"What a splendid idea!" Nana said and hugged Nicole. "But it will be a very, very long ride in the car."

"I don't mind that, Nana. I want to see your island and your house! Besides, we can sing and tell stories on the way."

As Nana and Nicole watched the red sun set, they planned the summer journey.

☙ ☙ ☙

As soon as Nana parked the car down the road from the old house,
Nicole scampered out to stretch her legs. "Oh, Nana, your house is so small!
Can we go inside? I want to see!"

The house did look a lot smaller than Nana remembered. "Small island,

small houses, Nicole. I'm sorry, we can't disturb the new owners. But we can walk along the beach."

So, hand in hand, they climbed down a rocky path to the water. The scent of sea roses blooming on the bank mixed with the tang of salt in the air. Seagulls screeched in the sky above.

As Nana and Nicole explored the beach, they filled their pockets with tiny periwinkles, sun-bleached clam shells, and sea glass.

Even though they found one beautiful lavender piece of sea glass and a few blue ones, most of the pieces were green, white, or brown. After a while, a disappointed Nicole said, "I wish we could find some *other* colors."

Then, at the same time, Nicole and Nana both saw it. There in the sand, still wet from the receding tide, gleamed a small piece of beautiful red beach glass.

"No, this can't be," Nana said aloud.

"Can't be what? Is this a jewel?" Nicole asked.

Nana reached down and picked up the glass. "No, it isn't a jewel, but this red glass reminds me of a story. Come, Nicole, let's find a good rock to sit on. You'll soon see why I have never told you this story. I think it happened when I was just about the age you are now.

"One summer day I was very restless—just as you sometimes get! School was out, and I couldn't think of anything interesting to do. So I wandered from room to room. When I came to the door of the parlor, I saw the sunlight splashing across the floor. It stretched up to the mantel, where, in its special place, the red vase gleamed. It seemed as if the vase were calling, 'Pick me up! Pick me up!'

"Now, I knew that playing in the parlor was not allowed. In fact, no one ever sat on the stiff-backed sofa and itchy chairs there except when company came to call. And the parlor was filled with things that break. 'Do not touch!' my mother must have reminded me a hundred times. 'That vase especially is off-limits to you. It was one of your great-grandmother's most prized wedding gifts.'

"But the vase was red—my favorite color. Like a very powerful magnet, it pulled me right into the room. And, of course, I could not resist picking it up.

"Using both hands, I carried the vase to the sunniest window. When I held it up, I realized I could still see the sky and sea. But through the crimson glass, everything looked different. White-feathered clouds, crisp blue sky, gray-green sea, and frost-tipped waves were now all softly shaded in rose and red. It seemed like magic. I could not put the vase down.

"Then, suddenly, something brushed my leg. I jumped. The vase crashed to the floor! Broken glass scattered everywhere!"

Nicole interrupted. "But what brushed your leg, Nana?"

"My cat, Minou. My naughty cat! I hurried to pick up the pieces of glass before my mother could see that vase broken on the floor.

"Being careful not to cut myself on the sharp edges, I quickly gathered the glass in the folds of my dress. I checked to see that my mother was busy in the kitchen and then sneaked by to get to the shore.

"It was a moon tide. That's what we called a tide that goes much lower

than usual. I had to walk very far out, past the spot where we usually dumped the cracked canning jars and chipped china cups. I climbed over the slippery rocks to reach the water's edge. With a huge sigh of relief, I tossed the broken glass into the ocean.

"Of course, my mother happened to dust that day. She noticed right away that the vase was missing, but she didn't blame Minou. It was all *my* fault!

"I got a terrible scolding and was sent to my room without any supper. I remember thinking about Humpty Dumpty. You know the rhyme about all the king's horses and all the king's men. Like Humpty Dumpty, that vase could never be put back together again. I felt sad and had a very hard time getting to sleep that night.

"After that summer, we moved to the city. And even though many years have passed, I have never forgotten about the red vase. Whenever I see a red sun rising, or setting, or red leaves in the fall, I think, If only . . . if only I had saved just one piece of that special red glass!"

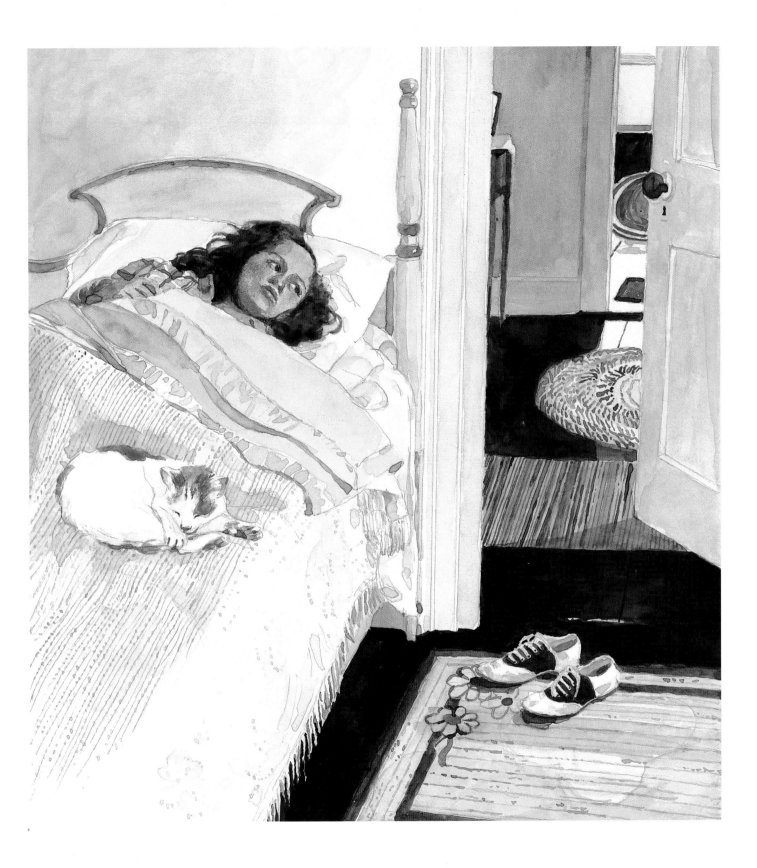

Nana held the red sea glass up to the sun. "I thought the sea would hide my mistake. But maybe the sea fooled me. You know, it's amazing how the sea can take a shard of jagged, broken glass and keep it for years, tossing and pounding it until it becomes sea glass, smooth and round. This red glass is frosted now, and I can't see through it. It can't give us the rose-colored world I saw through the magical red vase. Yet the sun makes it glow in a wonderful new way. Here, Nicole—hold it up and see for yourself."

Nana got up and pulled Nicole to her feet. "Come. Let's search some more. Perhaps we can find some other pieces of red sea glass and maybe more of your favorite blue. We'll collect enough to make sun-catchers. Then, when sunshine lights the sea glass in the window at home, we will always remember this special place and this time together—just you and me."

What Is Sea Glass?

Sometimes nature has a way of transforming trash into something beautiful, and so it is with the broken glass people throw away at the edge of the sea. Worn smooth by time and tides, sea glass (or beach glass) can be found buried in the sand, caught in the crevices of the rocks, or just lying on the surface of the beach. The best pieces look like precious stones. They gleam when they are wet.

Part of the fun is trying to guess what the glass used to be. White, green, and brown sea glass comes mostly from soda, wine, and beer bottles. Those colors are the easiest to find. Lavender and aqua glass often comes from very old bottles or canning jars. It is much harder to find. If you are lucky, you may find blue glass from an old medicine bottle or cold cream jar. And red glass, perhaps from a vase like the one Nana broke or the tail light of an old car, is special because it is very rare.

Today, more and more items are made from plastic. People also are more careful not to throw their trash in the ocean. This means that sea glass is getting harder to find.

Even though it will never have the value of silver or gold, sea glass is fun to collect and display, either wet or dry, in a jar in a sunny window. Many items can be made from sea glass, too—jewelry, sun-catchers, paperweights, and mobiles, to name just a few. Of course, a very smooth, rounded piece can just be carried in a pocket and used as a worry stone in the same way many Greeks use worry beads.

How To Make Your Own Sea Glass Sun-Catcher

Sun-catchers hanging in a window will capture the sun's rays and remind you of a sunny summer day at the beach, even in January.

First find a piece of sea glass about three inches across. This will be the base. White glass is best because it lets the most light shine through.

Select several very small pieces of well-worn colored sea glass to glue on top of the base piece. Plan your design before you glue them down.

Use a type of glue that will dry clear. Apply only a small amount so that you do not get extra glue squishing out between the pieces of colored glass. A cotton swab or toothpick is handy to wipe off any extra glue.

When the glue is completely dry, wrap a transparent line around the edge of the sun-catcher and tie a secure knot. (Clear nylon thread or fishing line work well.) Add a loop for hanging. Craft stores sell clear plastic suction cups with hooks for hanging items directly on the window glass.

You can also use a piece of clear plastic for the base piece if you want your sun-catcher to be less heavy—for example, if you plan to use it as a Christmas tree ornament. Punch a hole near one edge for hanging. (Just be careful not to cover the hole with glue when you attach your pieces of sea glass.) Use a type of glue made especially for plastic so that your pieces of sea glass will stay stuck!

[My book, *Beachcombing and Beachcrafting,* published by Wescott Cove Publishing Co. in 1989, explains how to make sun-catchers and other items from sea glass, shells, driftwood, and other things that wash up on the beach.]

FOR MY FAVORITE BEACHCOMBING COMPANIONS:
KRISTEN, CORI, CASEY, ERIC, MARCUS, AND SARA
—A. W. D.

FOR TREG AND MARION
—M. B. O.

Story copyright © 1999 by Anne Wescott Dodd
Illustrations copyright © 1999 by Mary Beth Owens

ISBN 0-89272-416-1

Printed in China through Four Colour Imports, Ltd.

4   2   5   3   1

Down East Books
P.O. Box 679
Camden, ME 04843
Book Orders: 1-800-685-7962

Dodd, Anne W.
    The story of the sea glass / Anne Wescott Dodd ; pictures by Mary
Beth Owens.
       p.   cm.
    Summary: When Nicole finds a beautiful piece of red sea glass on
the beach, her grandmother Nana tells her a story from her own
childhood of a broken red vase, which may have been the origin of
this sea glass. Includes information about sea glass and
instructions for making a sea glass sun-catcher.
    ISBN 0-89272-416-1 (hardcover)
    [1. Glass Fiction. 2. Beaches Fiction. 3. Grandmothers Fiction.]
I. Owens, Mary Beth, ill. II. Title.
PZ7.D66245St 1999
[Fic]—dc21
                                            99-13120
                                              CIP